For Josephine Pagan with love — R. S.

To Jay, for all your help and encouragement —
this one's for you — T. W.

First U.S. Edition 1996

First published in Great Britain by ABC, All Books for Children, a division of
The All Children's Company Ltd., 33 Museum Street, London WC1A 1LD, England

ISBN 0-316-77243-7

Library of Congress Catalog Card Number 94-73588

10 9 8 7 6 5 4 3 2 1

Published simultaneously in Canada
by Little, Brown & Company (Canada) Limited

Printed in Singapore

Who Likes Wolfie?

Story by **Ragnhild Scamell**
Pictures by **Tim Warnes**

Little, Brown and Company
Boston New York Toronto London

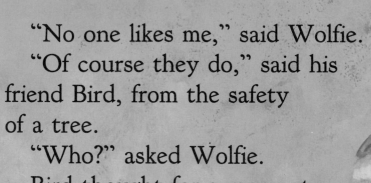

"No one likes me," said Wolfie.
"Of course they do," said his
friend Bird, from the safety
of a tree.
"Who?" asked Wolfie.
Bird thought for a moment.
"Well, there's...um...and..."

"You can't think of anyone,
can you?" said Wolfie sadly.
"No one likes me."

Bird felt sorry for his friend, but it wasn't really surprising that no one liked Wolfie. He looked too fierce.

"I like you," said Bird firmly. "And I'd like you even better if you smiled a bit more."

Wolfie looked up and gave Bird a big smile. "Like this you mean?" He beamed.

Bird almost slipped off
his branch when he saw
Wolfie's sharp white
teeth. He didn't mean
to, but he quickly jumped
onto a higher branch.

"Perhaps it's better if you don't smile," said Bird. "What about doing something that is really, really nice?"

"I can sing," said Wolfie. "Is singing really, really nice?"

"Yes," said Bird. "I'm very good at singing myself."

That night, as the moon began to rise over the snowy slopes, Wolfie marched with his brothers and sisters to the top of the highest hill. He stretched his neck toward the moon.

"Auoohuu," he howled,
just to test his voice.
"Auoohuu," echoed his brothers
and sisters.
Their voices drifted over the slopes.

Wolfie led his family to where
Bird was trying to sleep. He craned
his neck back as far as it would go and
began to sing.

It's so hard to be good when they think you're bad.
They say I'm bad, and it's making me sad.
I want to be good,
And I know I could—
But it's hard to be good when you're bad.

"Baahaahad—aaoohuuoou," harmonized his
brothers and sisters.

"Stop that racket!" shouted Polar Bear from his cave. "There are bears here trying to sleep!"

But Wolfie didn't hear him. He was spellbound by the round silvery moon, and he just had to sing.

I'll be glad when they don't think I'm bad.
On that day I'll no longer be sad.
It's so hard to be good,
Though you know that you could
If they'd tell you, "You aren't so bad."

"Baahaahad—aaoohuuoou," harmonized his brothers and sisters.

When the final note had
been sung, Wolfie turned
and smiled at Bird, who was
still sitting in the tree. His big
sharp white teeth glistened
in the light from the
silvery moon.

"Right," said Bird. "Yes, very um . . . nice."
"Really, really nice?" asked Wolfie.
"Not bad," said Bird.
"I'll do it again, if you like!" said Wolfie.
"No, no," protested Bird.
But Wolfie did it again, and as he sang, a
warm feeling of happiness spread through him.

By the time Wolfie had finished, Polar Bear and his family, some reindeer, and quite a few rabbits had gathered around him. They looked stunned from lack of sleep.

"I think they're getting to like me and my songs," Wolfie confided to Bird.

Just then, a beautiful shadowy creature
appeared from the woods. Wolfie saw her
at once. His heart beat faster, and he howled
his song to the moon with such feeling that
Bird had to bury his head under his wing.
"Auoohuuoou!"

Never had Wolfie seen anyone
as beautiful as the creature. As she
walked up the snowy slopes, her coat
sparkled in the moonlight. Her eyes
shone with a yellow light, and her
razor-sharp white teeth glistened so
perfectly that he was afraid her soft
pink tongue would be hurt.

Polar Bear, the reindeer, and the
rabbits stood aside. They, too, had
seen those sharp white teeth.

She didn't stop until she was right
beside Wolfie. She smiled at him, and
his chest swelled with pride.

"That was really nice," she said.

"Really, really nice?" asked Wolfie.
"Really, really nice," she said.
"Just like you!"

For a moment, Wolfie was so happy
that he couldn't speak.
   "This is a verse just for you," he told her.
   And, as he stretched his long neck
toward the moon, Wolfie knew at last
that someone liked him.

You make me know I'm not so bad.
That's so nice, I've stopped feeling sad.
It's a joy to be good —
You just knew that I could.
For you I'll be good, never bad!